# Hidden

**Randi Stroyan**

Copyright © 2024 Randi Stroyan

First Edition

PAGE PUBLISHING
Conneaut Lake, PA

First originally published by Page Publishing 2024

ISBN 979-8-89315-657-7 (pbk)
ISBN 979-8-89315-674-4 (digital)

Printed in the United States of America

# Contents

# Chapter 1

*Minni-Lane Rose*

Many years ago, deep in the forest, there lived a girl unknown to the world. She had long blonde hair, bright blue eyes, and dark pink cheeks. She lived in a shack hidden by the river. One morning, she was outside gathering veggies from her garden when a young man out hunting ran into her.

"Hello, ma'am, are you lost?"

She replied, "No, sir," and tried to run away.

"Ma'am, please stop. What is your name?" he asked very politely as he reached for her to come back.

"Minni," she replied. "What is yours?" She tried to hide her face with her long blonde hair.

"My name is Anthony, ma'am. May I ask what a girl like you is doing hidden in the woods?"

Before she could answer, an older man called out, "Minni, Minni, where are you?"

The girl looked at Anthony and said, "I must go, and you must leave and never come back, sir." She ran like no other without looking back in fear that her father would be angry with her.

As she approached her father, she tried to hide her face, fearing he would find out about Anthony wandering in the woods. She said, "Father, I'm sorry I was out grabbing all the vegetables before the storm comes. Is everything okay?"

"No, it's not, Minni. It's hunting season, and you do not need to be seen by anybody. You need to always stay nearby."

"Why, Father? Why do I always hide? I'm sixteen now, and I want to explore the world," she replied.

"No, Minni, you must stay here near me, where you are safe, and I can keep the promise to your mother."

As she turned to speak another word, her father stood tall and, with much force in his voice, said, "End of discussion, Minni-Lane Rose Feathers. I will not hear another word." As she stepped back from her father, he looked at her in deep thought and told her to go in the house and prepare dinner.

Later that night, she sat at the table, trying to keep quiet, knowing it would be a mistake to upset her father. The last time she tried talking about traveling elsewhere to explore the world, her father grabbed her hand and placed it over the fireplace, leaving Minni with third-degree burns. She sat quietly, awaiting to be spoken to first. As she waited patiently, she stared into her glass in deep thoughts. She asked herself all types of questions: *Why is Father so angry with me? What is he protecting me from? Why can't I leave? Is he really my father?*

At that moment, she looked at her father. Her father cleared his throat.

"So, Minni, besides disobeying me today, did you do what you needed to for your chores?"

"I have done everything today, sir. And Father, I do apologize about wandering close to the roads. I promise it will never happen again." She then had a thought about Anthony, the man she met earlier that day. She thought for a minute and then decided not to tell her father about him, fearing she would be punished. "Father, may I have permission to go to bed? I must lay down. I have chores to get done early in the morning."

Her father looked up and said, "You have my permission." He smiled and said, "Good night," to his daughter as she walked into her room.

As she lay there in her bed, she thought about how handsome Anthony was, how intrigued she swas by his dark brown hair, his beautiful brown eyes, and his smile that could light up a whole room.

*I really hope I see him again,* she thought. *I have so many questions like how the world is, is it better than her shack in the woods"* She fell asleep holding on to her pillow.

The next morning, when she woke up, she looked out the window into the woods, wondering if Anthony was out there hunting again. She stepped out of her room into the kitchen, where her father was sitting, drinking his coffee and reading an old magazine (that he had read a million times) waiting on Minni to fix breakfast.

"Father, we are out of eggs. When are you planning to visit town again for more food and magazines and a few more items that we need? It's been a month since you last went.

Her father looked up at her and said, "Yes, Minni, my dear, I shall go today."

"Great, Father, I will pack you a few things to throw away while you are out."

When her father traveled, he went eight hours away from their shack in the woods, hoping no one would recognize him. He put on a dark pair of sunglasses with his fishing hat and turned and said, "I will be back tomorrow before the sun sets. Do not wander in the woods."

"Yes, Father, I will always stay near home, sir."

She looked out of the window as her father untarped his light blue Chevy truck and watched him drive away. "Good, Father has left. I need to do my chores." She started with cleaning up the kitchen after breakfast. She started to prepare dinner as she just finished hand-washing their clothes and hanging them to dry. "Tomorrow I shall fold the laundry and put it away and then I'm going to go see if Anthony is around again."

The next day, she took her basket and headed to her garden. There was no sign of anybody being there. She stood there confused, wondering if maybe her father had run into Anthony and told him to leave his private property. She gathered all the veggies she needed and wrapped them in a towel in her basket. She headed back to her house to finish up, and she was ready to have her dinner.

A few days later, her father came home.

"Father, where have you been? It's been four days. Are you hurt? Is everything okay?"

"Yes, Minni, my dear. I wanted to see if you would obey and stay near. I'm proud of you, and for that, I brought you home some new shoes and a chocolate bar."

Thrilled, Minni jumped up in excitement. "Thank you, Father, thank you so much!"

Her father looked at her with a big smile and said, "You're welcome, Minni, my dear. Now take these bags and put away the food and start my dinner."

"Yes, Father." She ran to the kitchen with a grin from cheek to cheek. It had been a while since her father got her chocolate or shoes. After dinner, she sat with her father by the fireplace and asked about her mother.

Her father stood up and told her, "Not tonight. I am tired from my trip. Maybe another time."

She nodded and looked down; her father never wanted to talk about her mother. All he would tell Minni about her was how bright her blue eyes were and how long her hair was and that she loved Minni so much, passing away when Minni was only two years old. She did not remember much of her mom, only the smell of her; her mother smelled like sweet honey.

She missed her mother so much. She always thought if her mother were there, then maybe her life would be different. She never complained because she knew her father did the best he could at raising her all by himself.

The days turned into weeks and months, and she started to wonder if Anthony was ever going to come back. But one hot summer, Minni had gone to the river to get a few buckets full of water, and there he was sitting there in his ripped sleeve shirt and blue jean shorts, fishing.

"Anthony, she said in a really loud voice.

"Minni, it's you. Where have you been? I have been looking for you since the first day I met you."

She looked down as she started to blush and replied, "I also have been looking for you. I was thinking that maybe you did not want to see me again. I'm happy you are here."

Anthony and Minni had been talking for hours. She never laughed the way she did with Anthony.

The sun was going down, and she stood up and said, "Oh no, I need to go. I can't have Father finding out that I met you."

She started running, and Anthony stopped her and said, "Can you meet me here tomorrow? I want to see you again. What is your full name?"

She turned and looked at Anthony and said, "Yes, I will meet you here tomorrow, and my name is Minni-Lane Feathers."

For months, they met down by the river every day. He would tell her about the town news, all the carnivals, and fun events the town put together. Anthony stared into Minni's bright blue eyes and asked, "Why are you here? What is your father keeping you from?"

"I don't know, Anthony, and I'm afraid to upset him if I ask." She was falling for Anthony, and she knew that was a conversation for her dad. Maybe then she could ask to move closer to town so she could be closer to Anthony, but the thought of her father punishing her was sitting in the back of her mind.

The next morning, she was preparing breakfast as her father walked into the kitchen and took a seat at the table. Her father stood up and asked, "Why are you always going down by the river?"

She looked up, shocked about the questions, and said, "I'm getting water to wash, and I go to get water."

Her father looked at her and said, "Do you really think that I'm not that smart? What is the reason? There has to be a reason!" he yelled at the top of his lungs. Her father stood up and threw the table across the room, wasting all the food that Minni spent all morning preparing. Minni ran out of the room, crying and terrified. Her father followed her in there, demanding to know.

Minni kept telling him about the same thing over and over, "I was getting buckets of water to wash."

Her father glared at her and walked away. Minni shut and locked herself in her room.

Minni was terrified to go see Anthony again; she was scared her father was going to follow her and forbid them from ever speaking again, so she kept her distance and did not go back to the river for months. She waited until it was time for her father to go back to town for supplies. Then and only then would she go see Anthony.

# Chapter 2

As Minni was lying in her room reading a book, her father walked into the room.

"Minni, write a list of things we need. I'm heading to town."

"Yes, Father," she said, standing up quickly to get her list, knowing the moment her father left she was going to see Anthony.

As her father drove off, she sat there staring out her window, waiting for the moment that she could head out to the river, hoping she would see Anthony. It had been a few long months of not being able to speak to him.

She hurried to the river, but Anthony was not there. She sat on the rocks, upset.

"Minni, you're here," said a voice in the background. There he was, standing tall in his camouflage hunting gear.

"Oh, Anthony, I'm sorry, but Father is questioning my whereabouts, and he must not find out about you."

Anthony rushed to her and grabbed her hand, pulling her close and slowly placing his lips upon hers. She slowly stood back, not knowing what to do. He looked at her, stared deep into her soul, and said, "I have feelings that I've never felt before, and I always need you near me. I love you, Minni."

Shocked and unaware of the feelings she had, she said, "I love you too, but Father would never allow it. I'm sorry, Anthony."

He then pushed his whole body against hers, ran his hands down her face, and proceeded to kiss her. He whispered, "Tell me to stop if you don't want this."

Minni then kissed him back and told him to go with her to her shack. "My father won't be back till dinnertime tomorrow. Stay with me here tonight."

Anthony agreed. Then they showed each other their love for one another.

The next morning, when Minni opened her eyes, Anthony was staring at her. He did not go to sleep; he would rather watch her sleep.

"Good morning, beautiful. How was your sleep?"

She smiled at him and said, "It was wonderful."

As she stood up and looked out the window, she said, "You need to leave right now. Father is back. Go now, out the back door."

Anthony jumped up and got dressed. He looked at Minni and asked, "Run away with me. We can start our own family. Please, Minni, I can give you a better life than this."

"Not now, my love. Within time. You need to leave now," she replied.

Anthony left and just ran until he was out of sight from her shack.

"Father, you are home so early."

"Yes, Minni, my dear. I went into the first town I could find, and I got everything we need for at least a month. With winter on the way, it's better to be prepared. Now go prepare a feast."

She walked into the kitchen and began chopping some vegetables. All she could think about was the night she had with Anthony, how he made her feel when he ran his fingertips across her whole body, how it felt with his body against hers when he held her.

Later that night, she stared out at the stars, wondering if she was going to see him again, imagining what her life would be like if she ran off with him.

"Minni, what is this? Answer me now."

Minni, barely waking up, heard her father. "What are you talking about, Father?"

In a hurry to leave, Anthony had left his pocket watch.

"Where did you get this from?"

"I've never seen that before, Father."

"Lies! All you ever do is lie after I spent your whole life taking care of you." Her father grabbed her by the arm and threw her into the wall. "Answer me, Minni."

She stood there with her eyes full of tears, not wanting Father to get angrier. She said, "I found it out by the road."

"What were you doing that far from the shack, Minni? I've told you multiple times not to go that way!" As he lifted his hand to slap her across her face, Anthony came in and yelled, "Take your hand off her now!"

"Anthony," she gasped. Her father yelled, "Who are you, and why are you in my home?"

"My name is Anthony Chester. Why do you lay your hands on Minni? She has done nothing wrong?"

"Who do you think you are, coming into my home, on private property, and telling me how to raise my daughter?" her father yelled.

"Father, stop! Please just stop!"

Her father pushed her away and said, "How dare you disobey me and ask me not to be angry!"

Minni asked Anthony to leave. Her father then yelled, "Yes, leave and never return."

Anthony, confused, agreed and said, "I will be back. I love you, and you will leave with me."

Her father reminded him that Minni was only just barely seventeen years old, and there was nothing he could do. "Now, Minni, start preparing my dinner."

As she finished preparing dinner, her father went into her room and screwed her windows shut. He walked back into the kitchen and said, "Now go to your room for the night without dinner and think about what you did."

"No, Father, I will not!" she yelled.

Her father grabbed her and pushed her into her room and locked her in there.

The next morning, her father informed her that they would be moving and to grab all her belongings that she wanted to keep.

"Why, Father? Why must we go? Please just let me stay. I love him."

"You know nothing about love. You are way too young. Now gather your things," he yelled.

As they were loading their belongings into the truck, she noticed a wooden chest with a lock on it. The lock was not closed, so she looked around, making sure her father did not see her looking in it. There were multiple articles on a missing girl named Annalee Shelby. Also in the chest was a birth certificate and a lot of money. Confused about what was going on, she ran inside and began writing a letter to Anthony. She placed it under her bed.

The letter read,

> Dear Anthony,
>
> My father is so angry he's forcing me to leave with him, and I have no clue where we are going. Also, I found a chest with articles on a missing girl named Annalee Shelby. I think he might have been involved in her disappearance. I really hope to see you again.
>
> Love, Minni-Lane

A few hours later, her father yelled, "Time to go, Minni."

She got into the truck and looked out the window toward her shack and thought to herself, *If I had never shown Anthony where I lived, I would not have to move. Why must I always disobey Father? Maybe he is right. Maybe I should listen.*

Lots of thoughts were going through her head as she laid her head on the window while they drove away.

They had left Maine three days ago and still had not found a place to go. Her father drove them into New York. He found a small town called Saranac Lake. Her father wanted to be close to the water as they were already used to being by the river her whole life. With all the big changes, they wanted something similar. As he approached a beautiful two-story house with a For Sale sign on it, he said, "You must stay in the car. I will go talk to the owner about buying this house."

She sat quietly. As she looked around, she thought to herself, *There are other houses nearby. There are other people around.* She smiled and thought, *Yes! Finally, am I going to be normal?*

Her father came back to the truck and informed her that he had bought the house.

"You can go inside now and decide what room you would like to make yours. When we are done unloading the truck, I will run to town and buy furniture and food."

Her father then firmly said, "Nothing will change. You will not be leaving the house for any reason."

She nodded and said, "Yes, Father, I understand."

She walked through the house. It had big bay windows, a bathroom, a kitchen, and a living room downstairs. Upstairs had three bedrooms and two bathrooms. After looking at the whole house, she decided she wanted the master bedroom. After her father thought about it for a few minutes, he agreed and allowed her to have that room. Later that evening, she took a long hot shower. That was something she had never experienced living in her shack in the woods. As she sat by her bedroom window, all she could think about was Anthony. How she missed him and wished to be with him, not knowing if she would see him again was killing her.

Back in Lewiston, Maine, Anthony also could not keep his mind off Minni's soft, sweet lips. Anthony went back to the shack. In anger at them being completely gone, he started hitting the walls and throwing all their belongings that they had left all over the place. Anthony looked down where her bed was and saw a note lying under there. He grabbed it and began to read.

*Who is Annalee Shelby?* he thought. *Why did they leave?*

Later that day, he started his research and he found out that Annalee went missing at two years old in 1995, and it was now 2010, and it also stated the girl would be seventeen now. He thought to himself, *Wait, Minni is seventeen, and she said she's been in that shack since she was two. Could it be? Is Minni actually Annalee?*

He immediately got ahold of the police and told them everything he knew about the unknown girl that lived in the woods, only four hours away from where the little girl Annalee was taken. Annalee had inherited her grandfather's fortune. Why did she go missing without any of her belongings or money at only two years old? *Where is Minni now? How can I find her?* Anthony drove himself crazy trying to figure all this out.

The most important question he asked himself was, *How can I find my sweet Minni? I will find you, and I will bring you home.*

# Chapter 3

Back in Maine, the search for Annalee Shelby continued. The police used all the traffic cameras and town's gas station cameras to see where Minni-Lane was going with her father. At this point, the police and all the townspeople were convinced that Minni was, in fact, Annalee, but the only way to know for sure was to find her and run a DNA test.

They were getting closer to finding her. They had their suspicion on her being in New York due to the timelines on all video surveillances. A week later, Anthony went to check on the investigation at the police station to see if they were getting closer to finding his sweet Minni-Lane. As he was standing there waiting for the investigator to take his visit, a tall, older lady walked in wearing a long blue dress. Her hair was long and blonde, and she had the same bright blue eyes as Minni. She approached the desk where Anthony was standing.

"Hello, young man. Are you the one that turned in the information on Annalee?" said the lady in a deep but soft voice.

"Yes, ma'am. My name is Anthony. May I ask your name?"

The lady looked up and down at Anthony and replied, "Yes, my name is Saralee Shelby."

At that moment, he knew that Minni was, in fact, Annalee. It was as if Ms. Saralee copied and pasted herself onto Minni-Lane.

After a while waiting for the integrator, Officer Channing stepped out of his office and called both Anthony and Ms. Shelby into the office.

Anthony immediately asked, "Have you found Minni?"

Ms. Shelby cleared her throat and replied with, "Her name is Annalee."

"I'm sorry, ma'am, but until we know for sure, I will continue to call her Minni," said Anthony.

She nodded and replied, "Okay, but I know that girl is my daughter."

At this point, Ms. Shelby had already seen videos of her with her father in stores when they stopped for bathroom breaks, and she knew the moment she saw her that, that was Annalee. Annalee took after her mother in every way.

After the meeting, Ms. Shelby approached Anthony and asked if he would attend lunch with her.

After a few moments, he replied, "Yes, ma'am, I suppose I can for Annalee. I would like to know more about her."

It was now summer, and they still had not found Minni's whereabouts. All the townspeople were involved in the search for Annalee, the girl who had been missing since she was two years old. Anthony never gave up on the search for his Minni-Lane. He knew the last area they knew where she was, was in a small town in New York, but suddenly, they didn't see her in any surveillance cameras, as if she fell off the planet Earth. So Anthony decided he would go there, knock on every door, and not rest until he found her.

*I will not give up. She will be eighteen soon, and I will marry my sweet Minni-lane*, he thought to himself.

He headed to town to gather all the supplies that he thought he might need for his travels and immediately headed on the three-day journey, hoping and praying he could finally find her and bring her home to her family. Ms. Shelby had given Anthony her phone number, and if he was to find her, her mother must have been the first to know before the police.

Back in New York, Minni was in her room reading when her father came in and said, "You will be eighteen soon, and it's almost been a year since we moved here. Is there something special that you want for your birthday?"

She replied, "Yes, Father, I want a television. I've never had one, and it would be nice to watch movies rather than read all the time. I really don't have much to do anymore since we left the woods."

He agreed, then he stood back and told her that they were almost completely out of money and that he needed to get a job so they could continue to survive. Minni offered to get a job as well, but her father told her no. His reason was that she was a lady, and her job was cleaning, cooking, and taking care of the household.

A few hours later, she knocked on her father's bedroom door and asked, "Father, where did you get all that money from that we have been living on my whole life?"

He looked up at her and said, "It was a gift years ago."

"Father, just tell me the truth, please."

"It is none of your business. You need to mind yourself. Just because we have moved and I allow you to do more doesn't mean you can get into other people's business."

Minni nodded, walked away, and said, "I'm tired, Father. I'm going to my room now." She went into her room and lay down.

A couple of days later, Anthony was getting closer to the last place Minni had been seen. From there, he was going to ask about the direction she had gone. As he approached the store, he saw a light blue Chevy truck that looked like her father's. He waited in his car to see who would come out. It was Minni's father that walked out of the store. He quickly wrote down the plate number and called it in for the plates to be run. He then started to follow the man in hopes he would see his sweet Minni-Lane Rose. Anthony followed him to a small car garage; it appeared that was where he was working.

He sat there patiently without taking his eyes off the truck. Then his phone rang. It was the investigator on the case calling and asking if he was sure this was the man he had seen at Minni-Lane's shack in the woods.

Anthony confirmed, and the officer said the plates came back in the name of Fred Feathers. As the officer was talking, Fred got into his truck and left. Anthony followed closely. Fred pulled into his driveway, and Anthony parked a couple of blocks away so he would not be caught by Fred, in fear he would take Minni and leave again. He finally found his sweet Minni and was not going to lose her again.

Anthony slept in his car and refused to leave. He was waiting for Fred to leave for work so he could go see if his Minni was in that house. Finally, Fred walked out the door and left. Anthony waited a few moments before approaching the door, just to make sure her father was not coming back. After waiting a little while, he walked up to the house and knocked on the door. He knocked a few times but got no answer.

Inside, Minni-Lane heard the knock but refused to answer, in fear it was her father testing her again. She looked out the window but did not see her father's truck, so she finally walked downstairs, and barely pulling the curtains back, she saw the backside of a man. Very hesitantly, she opened the door. Her eyes lit up when she saw her love standing in front of her.

"Anthony!" she shouted and jumped into his arms. "How did you find me?" she asked.

Anthony then told her about the town thinking she was the missing girl, Annalee Shelby and that her mother was alive and looked exactly like her. The only way to know for sure was to get her back in town to do a DNA test.

"I can't," she said as she stepped away from Anthony. "I'm sorry, but Father will never allow it."

"You have been kidnapped," Anthony said in a high, firm voice. "We're not even sure if he really is your father. The police are coming to arrest your father, and you need to go back."

After thinking it over, she agreed and went upstairs to pack her bags.

Upstairs, she was in deep thought. Not wanting to upset Father, she decided to write a letter to him, warning him about everything. When she came downstairs, Anthony was on the phone, informing the police that he had found Minni-Lane. Before hanging up, he confirmed that they were both on the way back to Maine and would see them in just a few days. Anthony grabbed her bags in a rush and told her they had to leave before her father got back. As they drove off, she looked out the window, wondering if her father would get her note in time.

Later that day, her father pulled into the driveway, excited about finally getting Minni her television. He shouted, "Minni, Minni, come here!" But there was no answer, so he walked upstairs and walked into her room, only to find all her belongings gone. He then saw the letter.

The letter read,

Dear Father,

Anthony came and got me. They tracked us down by video surveillance on our way here. They ran your plates, and they know who you are. They are coming to arrest you. Do not get in that truck.

Love,
Minni-Lane Rose

Her father knew this might happen, so he went to his safe and grabbed a fake ID and passport. He went into his garage, where he had a red Volkswagen registered under the name Fred Luis. It was also the name on his fake ID and passport. He grabbed what he could and started driving. A couple of blocks away, he passed six police cars heading to his house. He got out just in time before his house was raided.

Fred headed to Mexico to hide out, but it was temporary. He would go back to get his daughter. He was worried that she would find out about her mother and never trust him again. *There is more to the story, Minni*, he thought to himself. All he could think about on his way to Mexico was the danger that Minni was now in.

# Chapter 4

A few days later, they arrived back in Maine and headed straight to the police station. Minni was nervous because she had no idea what was going to happen. As they walked in, the whole police station stood up and greeted the unknown girl. Officer Channing approached Minni and informed her what they had to do for now. He said, "Hello, Minni, I'm the investigator on your case. My name is Officer Channing. We will need to do fingerprints and a mouth swab to see who you really are."

Scared and shy, she replied with, "Yes, Officer."

They took her to the back and started the process.

Anthony waited in the front of the building for Minni to finish everything she needed to do. Ms. Saralee Shelby walked into the police station and ran directly to Anthony.

She asked, "Where is she? I must see her now! I told you to call me before the police. Why didn't you listen?"

At the top of her lungs, she yelled, "Where is Annalee? I need to see my daughter."

An officer walked out of his office to see what the issue was. "What is going on?" he firmly asked.

Ms. Shelby demanded to see her daughter at once. The investigator said that she was busy and that Ms. Shelby needed to relax and take a seat, or she would need to leave. After giving him a dirty look, she agreed to settle down.

An hour later, Minni-Lane walked out from the back and ran to Anthony. She grabbed him and would not let him go. She was scared. She had never been around this many people. She had only ever known her father and Anthony. It was so much for her to take in at once.

"Annalee?" asked Ms. Shelby.

Minni turned to look at the lady, confused. She walked toward her and said, "My name is Minni-Lane Rose Fethers."

Ms. Shelby replied, "If you are my daughter, your name is Annalee Rose Shelby."

Minni then said, "Well, I'm not sure if I am, so right now, I will answer to my name, Minni."

In shock that someone spoke to her that way, Ms. Shelby nodded and then asked, "What is your birthday?"

"October 18," Minni replied.

Ms. Shelby sighed and then said, "Well, my Annalee's birthday is also October 18. Is this a coincidence?" she asked.

"We will find out soon," said the investigator. "For now, you should all go home."

Ms. Shelby stood up and said, "Okay, Annalee—oh, sorry, I mean, Minni—you should grab your belongings from Anthony's car and come with me."

"No," said Anthony. "She does not know you. She will stay with me."

Ms. Shelby disagreed and reminded him that for another month, Minni was still a minor and should be with a guardian.

"Um, well, I don't have a guardian considering I left my father, and we have not gotten the results of the DNA test," said Minni. "For now, I will stay with Anthony, ma'am."

Unhappy and frustrated, Ms. Shelby stormed out the door.

"Let's go home," said Anthony, and they left the building. The drive to his house was long because he lived out of town.

When they arrived, Minni stared out the window in disbelief. They pulled into a mansion where he stayed with his whole family. Minni had never seen a house this big before. It was like seeing something in a movie (if she had ever seen a movie before).

"Wow, look how beautiful this is," said Minni.

Anthony smiled and said, "Well, I'm glad you like it. Are you ready to meet my family? They have been ready to meet you for over a year now, since that first day I met you."

Unsure what to say, she replied, "Sure."

As she walked in, she was ambushed by lots of people.

"Hello, I'm Anthony's sister, Bailey. You must be the famous Minni-Lane the whole town is talking about?"

"Yes, I mean, I guess," replied Minni.

Anthony giggled and said, "Minni, this is my family." He pointed at everyone. "This is my mother, Angela, my father, Andrew, and my little brother, Kevin. Don't be scared. They don't bite."

The whole family laughed.

"Now," said Anthony's father, "are you hungry? Would you like dinner?"

Minni said, "Sure, what can I do for preparations?"

Mr. Chester laughed and said, "Nothing, Minni. We have cooks and butlers, even maids. You will never again have to lift a finger while you are here."

Minni was very confused because she was always taught that the woman in the home is to take care of the household. She looked at him and said, "Are you sure? I'm very good in the kitchen."

"No, silly, you should come with me, and I will show you your room," said Bailey.

Minni walked up to Anthony and asked, "Why can't I stay in your room?"

Anthony explained that his family was old school and very strict. "We are not yet married, and you are still underage. But don't worry, you have your own room, and no one will bother you. Well, maybe my sister. She's probably going to bug you." He giggled and stood there as Bailey and Minni walked upstairs to her room to freshen up. She walked in and looked around at how beautiful the room was. It had huge windows with dark burgundy curtains, a king-size bed with a canopy around it, also with dark burgundy curtains, and its own bathroom.

"Wow," Minni said as she continued looking around.

Bailey said, "Um, you look about my size. Let me go grab you some clothes so you can clean up before dinner."

"No, that's okay," said Minni. "I do have my own clothes."

"No, ma'am," said Bailey. "It's really not a problem. I have way too many clothes I barely even wear. It would be nice to see someone wearing them."

Minni nodded, knowing that Bailey would not take no for an answer. "Thank you so much," said Minni as she walked into the bathroom to draw a bath.

Bailey returned with a maid carrying clothes, towels, and all the things she would need to freshen up.

The maid looked at Minni, smiled, and said, "I go by Sue. I've been assigned to be your personal maid. Anything you need, just let me know. I will be right outside the door and will help you get dressed when you are ready."

Minni nodded and got in the tub (also something she had never seen or experienced in life).

After she was done getting ready for dinner, she met Anthony at the bottom of the stairway. She was wearing a dark green evening gown. As she got to Anthony, she asked, "Do they always wear fancy clothes for dinner?"

Anthony giggled and replied, "Yes, get used to it, my love."

Minni smiled and said, "I will try. I'm just more of a basic girl. I never thought I would be in a situation like this. I didn't even know this kind of lifestyle existed."

They walked into the kitchen and joined his family for dinner. They all got to know each other and enjoyed Minni's presence.

In Mexico, Fred, Minni's father, was staying in a hotel. He thought about Minni every day, wondering how she was, if she was okay, and if she had met her mother yet. He was sitting on the bed watching the news on the whole story of the girl who had been missing and the story of the girl hidden in the woods. It was all over; this story had hit internationally. It was the headline of the month. "Is Minni-Lane actually Annalee?"

Her father shook his head and said, "Oh, Minni, my dear, what have you done?"

Back in Maine, Minni was having a great time. She and Anthony were going on a nice stroll on his property when Anthony's phone rang. It was the investigator.

"Is Minni with you?" asked Officer Channing.

"Yes," Anthony replied as he handed the phone to Minni.

"Hello, Ms. Feathers, I need you to come to the station. Your results are in."

"Yes, sir," replied Minni. "We will be there shortly."

They went to the police station, and Officer Channing greeted her at the door. He asked if she would be okay if he called and informed Ms. Shelby about their visit.

Minni asked if he did not because she still really did not want to be around a lot of people. Officer Channing agreed with her decision, and they went to his office.

"Well, Ms. Minni-Lane, you are, in fact, Annalee Rose Shelby."

Shocked, Minni looked at Anthony and said, "This is like something I have read in a book. I can't believe it's actually my life." She quickly asked, "Is Fred really my father?"

The officer replied he was not sure at all. "We would have to call in your mother to question your father."

Again, Minni was not ready for all that, so she decided to leave for now to try and comprehend everything.

The next morning, Anthony woke up to fifteen missed calls from an unknown number.

"Hello," said Anthony as he answered the phone.

"Hello, this is Ms. Shelby. The station has called and informed me that Minni is my daughter, Annalee."

Anthony asked her to give Minni some time to comprehend everything before she agreed to formally meet her mother. In anger, Ms. Shelby yelled, "No, I am her mother, and I have not been able to see her in sixteen years," and she demanded to see her now. After talking with Anthony, Ms. Shelby calmed down and tried to understand where her daughter was coming from. She agreed to wait until Minni was ready.

Later on, Anthony asked Minni if there was anything she wanted to do that she had never done before. Very excited, she jumped up and said, "Yes, I want to watch a bunch of movies and eat junk food till my teeth fall out!"

Anthony laughed as if he had never laughed before and said, "Okay, let's do it!"

He took Minni to their outdoor home theater, and they watched movies and enjoyed their night. Anthony was the only person she trusted and wanted around her at the time. She just kept looking at him, still in shock at how fast her life was changing and how lucky she was to have ever met Anthony.

# Chapter 5

It had been months since Minni-Lane had returned to Maine. Minni still refused to surround herself with anyone other than the Chester family; she stayed hidden in the mansion. She knew eventually she would need to see her mother. She was now eighteen years old, so she felt she was an adult and should not have to obey her parents anymore. She had enough of that her whole life in the woods with her father. She wanted a relationship with her mother, but she kept thinking to herself, *There must be a reason that my father took me and ran. Is she a bad person?*

Anthony knocked on Minni's door. "Minni, are you in here?" he asked as he slowly opened the door.

"Yes," she replied. "Can I help with anything?" she asked as she walked toward him.

"No, Minni. I am just here to let you know that my father is throwing what we call a ball. It is tonight. Wear something nice. My father has invited all the townspeople. This is your returning-home party for my family and me."

Before Minni could say anything, Anthony gently grabbed her hand and said, "It is time, Minni. You have hidden your whole life. It is time we put that in the past so you can continue and start living your life."

Minni agreed and asked Anthony if he could send up her maid, Sue, and his sister, Ms. Bailey. He agreed and walked out of her room.

All three of the women were going through many gowns.

"Ugh, you must look perfect," said Bailey. "This is your first party, and everyone has been waiting to meet the unknown girl."

"I am not the unknown girl anymore. I am Annalee, the missing girl, and I am just not too excited to meet everyone, including my mother." She looked at the maid and said she preferred to be called Minni-Lane.

Both ladies agreed she should be called whatever Minni wanted, and they informed her that they would let that be known at the party as well. As Bailey and Sue got ready to leave Minni's room, Anthony walked in.

"How are you doing?" he asked. "Are you still nervous? I promise I will not leave your sight, and if it begins to be too much, we will leave."

"How?" asked Minni. "We live here, and the party is also here." They both giggled because that was the first time Minni even tried to make a joke, and it was terrible. Anthony pulled her close and wrapped his arms around Minni and reassured her everything was going to be fine.

"I must get ready," said Anthony.

Minni replied, "Me too," in a low scared voice.

"I will meet you down there soon," said Anthony. Minni nodded and closed the door behind him.


A few hours later, it was party time. Minni slowly walked down the stairs to greet her love, Anthony. Anthony looked up and saw his Minni walking down the stairs. Her hair was in a beautiful bun, with curls hanging out. She had a perfect amount of natural makeup on, and she was wearing a long black gown with black heels. On her wrist was a diamond bracelet, and on her neck was a matching necklace that Bailey had given her. All Anthony could think of was how beautiful she was. Minni looked down at Anthony in his gorgeous black tuxedo and just smiled. She was still in shock that this was now her life.

"Hello to all," said Andrew Chester (Anthony's father). "Welcome to the Chesters' ball. This night is to help celebrate the return of Annalee Rose Shelby, but in respect for her, we shall all continue to call her by the name she knows and grew up with, Minni-Lane Rose Feathers. Now if we can all give her a round of applause."

The whole room got noisy with people clapping for Minni. Minni nervously smiled and held on tighter to Anthony's arm as they walked further into the room.

"So are you going to continue to ignore my existence?" said a voice behind Minni.

As Minni turned to look, she saw her mother, Saralee. She stepped back and said, "No, I am sorry. I am just still trying to get used to my living arrangements."

Saralee looked at Minni up and down and said, "Well, you are my daughter, and I've already missed so much of your life. You should be living with me."

Minni politely said, "I am sorry, but I know nothing about you. I was always told that you were dead. There must be a reason my father told me that. Can you answer why he did that?"

Saralee took a deep breath and said, "Well, my darling, I am not sure that this Fred Feathers is even your father. Your father's name was James Rials. He left when you were just a baby."

Minni looked confused and asked, "Why would he just abandon his child?"

Saralee said, "Well, my father told him that he needed to leave. My father, your grandfather, thought that James was a bad influence on me, so we were forbidden to even speak. So I can guarantee that whoever this man was that took you was not your father. Only your grandfather and I even know who he was, and after you went missing, I did try to find him, and I found out that he is the one that is dead."

Minni's eyes filled with tears, and she ran outside to the balcony to clear her mind. Anthony ran after her.

Anthony stood there in silence as he held Minni while she cried in his arms.

"How can this be?" said Minni. "I do not believe this. He is the only father I have ever known, and I refuse to believe what Ms. Saralee is saying. Can this be true? But why would he take me when it only inconvenienced his life more having to raise me and to have to be hidden his whole life?"

After much thought, Anthony pulled her out of his arms so he could grab her face and look into her eyes and said, "We can only find out the truth if we find Fred."

She nodded and said, "I feel like I have angered him. There is no way that he will come back or even talk to me, and I'm not even sure if I want to talk to him. I'm so confused. I must lie down for a little while."

Anthony grabbed her hand and asked if she would stay just a little longer. Anthony said, "I have a surprise. Will you continue to stay on my arm just for a little while longer? If you need more time to clear your head, we can stay out here for a little bit longer."

Minni nodded and hugged Anthony while she said, "You are the only thing that I am sure is real in my life."

Moments later, Anthony's mother, Angela Chester, walked outside and asked if the two of them would join everybody inside for a toast. They agreed and walked back inside as Minni wiped her tears away. They came inside, and a few people stood tall and said wonderful things about Minni-Lane.

Anthony then grabbed the microphone, and he got on one knee with a beautiful diamond ring and said, "Minni-Lane Rose Feathers, you are everything I want for my life. You are the most beautiful, brave, smart, amazing woman that I have ever laid my eyes on. Will you do me the honor of marrying me?"

The whole party smiled and cheered.

"Yes," Minni shouted, "that is one thing that I know for sure is real in my life. I will marry you, Anthony Chester."

Everyone congratulated the couple before leaving. Still in shock, Minni smiled, looked at Anthony, and leaned in for a kiss.

Saralee walked up to them, interrupting their moment, and said, "Well, I see you have no problem moving on with your life, pretending as if your mother does not exist. I beg of you to give it another thought and join me once at least for dinner. I really would love to get to know you, and your sister, Lillyann, would also love to meet her older sister."

"My sister?" said Minni. "Wow, that is amazing. I will not make promises, but I will think about it."

But in Minni's mind, she did not have a good feeling about Saralee, and she was always told, if something does not seem right, it usually is not.

In Mexico, Fred (Minni's father) was plotting and planning a way to get to Minni so he could tell her everything that he was keeping from her. He knew the police would always be near Minni since they had not yet found him. He started going through his wooden trunk that had a hideaway on the bottom. He went through documents and letters, trying to figure out if he had enough proof against Saralee that could at least keep him from going to jail until he could talk to Minni. He pulled out Minni's real birth certificate and his fake death certificate.

No one knew that James Rials had faked his own death so that he could take his daughter and not get caught. He knew that he would be the first person they looked for when she went missing. He thought to himself, *Minni, I hope you are doing well. Please stay away from Saralee. Minni, my dear, I was only trying to protect you. I hope one day you will understand and forgive me. My sweet girl, I will find you again!*

Her father never stayed at the same hotel. He knew that they would be looking for him, so he kept his distance from towns and stayed hidden using his fake identity. He eventually looked for work so that he would have enough money to go back and get his precious daughter. Not a night went by that he did not think about her and wished that he would have moved them years ago from that shack in the woods, but he knew it was too late to even be mad at himself. Now he made it his mission to go back to Maine and lure his daughter away from everyone and once again kidnap her.

Back in Maine, Minni also was thinking about her father, wondering if he was going to come back and try to take her away too. But deep down, she still felt that Saralee had something to do with it and her father was only trying to protect her from the worst.

As she lay there thinking of her father, it was storming. She began singing a lullaby that her father used to sing to her when it stormed. It helped get her through every storm, she thought to herself. He had his moments, but he did try and be a normal, loving father. *Maybe if I had not always misbehaved, my father could and would have controlled his anger, and I would not have been abused.* But then she thought, *Or not. I was just a child. I needed his love. He is the only person I knew before Anthony came into my life.*

She fell asleep singing, "The storm will not last, it will soon fade. I will always be here to protect you till my very last day."

# Chapter 6

Minni-lane was not raised as a typical girl. She was raised in the woods, and her father brought her up as if she was from the 1900s. She had to speak, dress, act, and behave in a certain way. After all those years, she had never had a real conversation with anybody. Adapting to the way society is now was a little hard on her, but she was managing it very well. Soon, she was going to be married to one of the wealthiest men in Maine. She no longer had to struggle. She no longer had to make a little bit last so long, and that was refreshing yet scary for her. Minni-Lane had no idea she was just as wealthy as Anthony, and soon she would find out.

One morning, Minni went on a walk. Somehow, she ended up in the woods (not where she was raised), but somehow, she felt calm and at home with nothing but trees surrounding her. She thought to herself, *I wonder if Anthony would agree to moving to a secluded area where it will be only him and I.* She kept that thought as she wandered around deeper in the woods. Minni heard Anthony calling for her so as quickly as she could she ran back to the mansion.

"Yes?" asked Minni as she approached Anthony.

Anthony asked why she was wandering in the woods, and in fear of him not understanding, she replied with, "Oh, I thought I had seen something. I was just investigating."

Anthony laughed and said, "Minni, you sure are silly. Most people don't go looking for things they are not sure of. That can be dangerous." Minni agreed and walked away from Anthony.

Anthony looked around, wondering what Minni was thinking, but before he could finish his thought, his phone rang. Anthony looked down and saw it was Saralee calling yet again to see if Minni would agree to meet. Anthony answered his phone.

"Yes, Saralee. Can I help you?"

"You know what I want, Anthony. Stop playing with me and put my daughter on the phone," said Saralee.

"She's not with me, ma'am. I will have her call you as soon as I see her."

Before Anthony hung up, Saralee said, "That's what you say every time," she mumbled before hanging up.

Anthony thought, *Maybe if I could get her to talk and spend time with her mother, she would stop acting so strange*, so he headed back to the house to try and convince her.

"Minni, can I have a word with you?" asked Anthony as he arrived back at the house.

Minni held her breath for a moment and said, "Of course, what's wrong?"

"Nothing is wrong, but your mother has been calling me a thousand times a day. Can you please agree to meet with her?" asked Anthony.

After giving it thought for a few minutes, she agreed. "Next Sunday, I will meet her. I'm busy this week going over wedding details with Bailey, but Sunday I shall make an appearance."

Anthony replied with, "Thank you. She's driving me crazy!"

"Minni, come now!" shouted Bailey from upstairs.

Back in Mexico, Minni's father was packing up to take this long trip back to Maine. He had cut his hair and dyed it a lighter color and shaved his beard in hopes of getting into town and getting Minni without being noticed. As he was packing his car, he kept saying to himself, "It will be okay. I can do this. She will be safe once again really soon."

He stopped at the store to buy a burner phone so he could look up Anthony's information and try to get a phone number to reach Minni. It was not hard for him to get the mansion's landline number. He called, and Sue answered, "Hello, Chester residence. May I help you?"

"Yes, I'm calling from the police station. Is Minni around? I have a few more questions about her father," said Fred, hoping that would work to talk to her.

"No, sir," replied Sue. "She is not home."

As she hung up, Minni was walking by and asked who had called. Sue told her, "No one important," because the Chester family was trying to protect Minni from all the drama, so Sue was told to keep all calls a secret, especially if it was a call from the police.

Minni had a new family and a new life, but deep down she still didn't feel right. She was trying to hide her feelings from everybody. Not ready to deal with her mother, she knew she had already agreed and needed to fulfill her promise for her image. She was getting ready to meet with Saralee.

She thought to herself, *At least I'm not going alone. My love will be there with me.*

Putting on her makeup, she kept thinking, *Why do I have a bad feeling about this? She is my mother. It's not her fault I was taken from her. I need to give her a chance.* Convincing herself everything would be okay, she called down to Sue asking if she could call her car.

Anthony and Minni arrived at the Shelby residence in their limo.

"Wow," she said as she looked out the window. "This mansion is just as big as yours," she said in disbelief that this was where she had originally come from.

Anthony explained to her how wealthy the Shelby family was and reassured her that this was her life and she did, in fact, belong here.

Saralee met them at the door. Saralee could not keep from smiling as she said hello and asked if she could have a hug. Minni agreed and reached for the hug.

Minni said, "The smell, your smell, I remember it. You smell like sweet honey."

Saralee giggled and said, "Yes, a lady must always smell good." She looked at Minni and said, "Well, shall we? There is someone who has been waiting a lifetime to meet you."

As they walked in, a young girl shouted, "Minni, you are here!" The girl ran down the stairs as if she had never run before.

"Hello, my name is Lillyann. I am your little sister."

Minni had never had a sister, so she grabbed her and hugged her and would not let go. Minni was finally starting to feel whole again. She knew the moment she saw Lillyann that she loved her and would do anything for her sister.

"Do I have any other siblings?" asked Minni.

"Oh no," said Saralee. "Well, let's go to the dining room, and I'll have the kitchen staff make us lunch."

They all walked into a huge dining room that had a table big enough to seat thirty people. It was a dark room with paintings of the family on the wall, very cozy and homey.

They all sat there for what felt like years, catching up on everything. The Shelby family finally got to hear how Minni was brought up. They felt pity for her. Saralee stood up and apologized to her for everything she had gone through and promised she would never have to go through that again. Minni was finally feeling comfortable, and that bad feeling that she once had faded away. She felt as if she belonged there with her family.

Anthony and Minni headed home, and as they drove off, Minni could not help but smile.

"Oh my goodness," she said as she turned to speak to Anthony. "That was amazing. I'm so glad I went. My sister looks just like me."

He nodded in agreement. "I'm glad you had fun, my sweet Minni, and there will be more times like this," he replied as he reached for her hand. "Now, Minni, how is all the wedding planning going? Do you think everything will come together by next fall?"

Minni replied, "Yes, and it's going to be beautiful."

As they continued talking about the wedding plans, Anthony's phone rang. It was the mansion calling to inform Anthony that they kept getting a call for Minni, and it was the police station. Anthony asked them to give him the number that had been calling. As Anthony went to dial, he thought to himself, *Mmm, this is an odd number*, but without thinking, he dialed it and handed the phone to Minni.

"Hello," said Minni.

"Hello, Minni. Don't hang up, and don't tell him that it's me on the phone. I need to talk to you and explain myself. The Shellby family is not what it seems."

Minni immediately hung up and told Anthony to save that number. Minni was sitting there thinking, *How did my father find me? Why does he want to talk to me, and why would he think I would ever want to talk to him?*

But she did, in fact, want to talk to her father. That's why she asked her love to save the number because she wanted to talk to him. She had so many questions, and she wanted answers.

# Chapter 7

The Chester residents loved throwing parties and celebrating. After a few weeks of convincing Minni-Lane, she finally agreed to an engagement party for Anthony and herself.

She thought, *Why not? It will prepare me for the actual wedding.*

There were people there all week preparing the yard because it was an outdoor-themed party. She stayed out of the way, hoping nobody would stop her and ask questions. She didn't feel the need to put her input in since Bailey was the one planning the party, and she was a bit of a control freak.

After everything came together, it was finally time for the party. Minni was upstairs getting dressed when Anthony walked in.

"Hello, my gorgeous bride-to-be."

Minni looked over at him, smiled, and asked, "Do we actually have to go to this thing? They're only throwing it to have a reason to have a party. Do I actually have to attend?"

Anthony giggled and replied, "Yes, this party is technically just for you."

"Ugh," said Minni as she brushed her long blonde hair.

"Minni, you are going to have to get used to this lifestyle," said Anthony as he reached down to kiss her forehead.

"I know, it's fine," she said as she continued to get dressed in her cream-colored evening gown with spaghetti straps. It was long and silk. Her heels were also cream-colored, with rhinestones on them. She was finally ready. Now to make an appearance at her party.

She was standing there, smiling next to Anthony as everyone stopped to greet them. After a little while, Minni was getting a little overwhelmed, so she walked around the mansion to the front.

"Finally, a break," she mumbled under her breath. As she was standing there, she looked over and saw a man with light hair and a clean shave. Not realizing who it was, she said, "The party is out back."

"Minni-Lane, I'm here to see you," said the man. Immediately she recognized the voice.

"Father, is that you?"

"Yes, Minni, my dear," said Fred as he walked closer.

"Stop right there! Don't come closer. Why are you here?" she shouted.

"Minni, you never called me back, and I need to explain everything to you," he said as he took a step closer.

"No!" Minni shouted again. "You took me from my family, from my home. What makes you think I want anything to do with you? And on top of all that, I know you are not my father. My father is dead!"

Fred looked at her and said, "Good, that is what your grandfather and I wanted everyone to think. Please, I have proof and documents to show you. I promise I just want to talk, that's it. Then if you're not convinced, I will turn myself in. But, Minni, you are in danger!"

After giving much thought, she agreed to speak to him, and she walked to his car with him. Before she would get in, she asked for his keys and threw them out toward the woods. Her father, in shock, actually thought that was pretty clever and laughed a little. He pulled out his wooden chest.

"I have already seen that, sir. I know my actual birth certificate is in there."

Fred looked over and said, "I bet you haven't seen this," and he pulled out a secret compartment in the chest.

"No, I haven't. What is that?" she asked.

Her father handed her his fake death certificate and multiple fake IDs and passports that he had for both of them, just in case they ever needed to leave in a hurry. He also showed her a photo of her father and mother holding Minni as a baby.

He said, "This was the first and last picture of you that we took as a family before your grandfather banned me from ever seeing you again. He thought I was just after his family's money, but it didn't take long for him to reach out to me."

Baffled, Minni asked why he reached out to him.

"Well, Minni, my dear, your grandfather, Jason Shelby, had fallen sick and found out some disturbing news about Saralee, and this was his attempt to protect you."

Minni looked down and asked, "What was the disturbing news about Saralee?"

"She wanted to kill you, Minni, my dear," said her father.

"No way! You're lying. She's my mother. I am her daughter. Why would she want to do that?" Minni asked.

"Here's the letter," Fred said as he handed it to her, but before she could read it, she heard the Chester family calling for her.

"I must go," she said. "I'm having a hard time believing this, but I will read this letter, and I will call you to explain more." Minni jumped out of the car and started running toward the party. Her father was about to leave when he realized his daughter had thrown his keys.

"Ugh," he said as he got out the car to find his lost keys.

Meanwhile, Minni was back at her party, trying to keep a smile on her face while talking to her guests. She kept thinking to herself, *How can I get out of here unseen so I can read this letter? Did my mother really try to kill me? Why would she want to hurt me? I was only two. Who in their right mind kills their own child?*

Frustrated, Minni told Anthony she needed to freshen up and she would be back. She didn't feel the need to tell Anthony about all this or that her father had shown up out of the blue.

Minni-Lane sat down, took a deep breath, and thought to herself, *Do I really want to read this?* After a few minutes, she began to read.

The letter read,

Dear James,

I'm writing you because I just found out that I am sick. I do not have much longer to live. I was preparing my will with my trusty butler, Kevin Foster, and my lawyer, Hyde Gammon. I am leaving my mansion, my company, and my entire fortune to Annalee Rose. Until she is old enough, Kevin is to run the business. My daughter, Saralee, has found out about all of this, and she is angry. My butler had overheard Saralee telling her friend that she was going to kill Annalee while she was sleeping so that she can inherit everything for herself. I will not have this. I need a favor from you. I am faking your death so they will not know it is you that has Annalee. I have bought a hidden property a few hours away under the name of Fred Feathers. I also pulled five hundred thousand dollars for the both of you to live off of; please use it wisely. I have given you multiple passports in case you ever get caught and need a new identity. When Annalee is of age, I need you to contact Kevin and Hyde. Until then, with Annalee gone, I don't know what is going to happen. Please raise her the correct way and keep her safe. I do not want Annalee to know about this, so in the meantime, tell her that her mother has passed and loved her very much.

With much love,
Jason M. Shelby

Minni-Lane was shocked at what she had just read, so she began her search for Kevin, the butler, and Hyde, the lawyer. She found out that both of them were fired after the death of Jason Shelby. Having no idea where to start, she asked Anthony to have his investigators search for these two men. Unaware of why she was looking for them (because Minni would not give a reason), he agreed and had the search for them begin.

Days had passed, and finally, they were getting somewhere. They found Kevin, and he agreed to meet with her. He'd known this day would come, and he was ready to fight this battle with her. As for Hyde, there was still no luck, but Minni would not give up. She knew she needed him the most. The search continued for weeks.

# Chapter 8

Furious with the whole situation, Minni needed to know why her mother wanted to do that to her, so she decided to confront her mother, but she wasn't sure how to. She thought to herself, *Father said Saralee is dangerous. Maybe I should wait.* But she just could not stop thinking about it. It bothered her to the core. Why would a mother want to harm her child over money?

After giving it a few days, she decided it was time to finally say something, but she didn't want to tell Anthony about it. Minni thought, *Why tell Anthony? I should wait. What my father said could be a lie, or maybe Saralee has a good explanation for why she would do that.*

As she was sitting there thinking about everything, Anthony walked in.

"Hello, my love," said Anthony. "How was your day so far? Did you get more wedding planning ready? It's getting closer."

"Yes, I have. Everything is ready," she said as she looked down.

Anthony rushed to her side and said, "Is everything okay? Are you still going to marry me? Why do you look so sad?"

"I'm fine, and yes, I'm still marrying you!" she replied. In her head, she was thinking about confronting her mother, but she reassured her soon-to-be husband that everything was okay.

It was the day Minni finally met with Saralee to ask her all the questions she needed to. Anthony offered to go with her, but Minni kept telling him no, that she needed mother and sister time alone. As she drove off in her personal car with her personal driver, Anthony was not feeling too good about letting her go alone, but despite that, he knew there was no stopping her. So Anthony texted her driver and made sure he kept a close eye on her.

As she pulled into the Shelbys' driveway, she felt something she had never felt before—lots of anxiety and stress. Her palms were sweaty; she could barely catch her breath. At that moment, she asked the driver to stop for a minute while she gathered all her thoughts. She was starting to get really nervous; she had no idea what to expect from Saralee after she asked her about what had happened. Her nerves took over her for a few moments, then she took a deep breath and told her driver to proceed. They pulled up to the door. Waiting out front was her mother (Saralee) and her sister (Lillyann). She got out of the car, and both of them rushed to her to give her a hug (before they all went inside for what they thought was a girls' day).

She waited to say anything because she was enjoying her time with her family. While they were eating their lunch, Minni-Lane looked up and softly asked her mother, "When I went missing, how long did it take you before you stopped looking for me?"

Saralee replied, "A year."

"So you only thought about me for a year, and you just stopped looking for me?" shouted Minni.

Saralee looked at her and asked, "Where is this coming from? We thought you were dead. We had no idea, and still have no idea, about who took you. Let the past be. We are here now. Let's just enjoy it."

Angry, Minni stood up and said, "No, Mother, let's not. I know you were going to kill me in my sleep, and Grandfather found out about it! That's why I was taken from my home, because my grandfather was trying to save me. He knew you were going to wait till he passed away and then kill me. Why? Just for my inheritance!"

"Stop, Annalee! Right now! You have no idea what you are talking about," said Saralee as she gave her the dirtiest look ever. "I did no such thing."

"I have proof," said Minni. "The man that took me was my father. Grandfather faked his death and printed a death certificate for my father."

"That's absurd," said Saralee as she went to stand up. "You're just trying to take your sister's and my money. What is wrong with you? You have turned greedy!"

"No, I haven't, Mother." Minni threw all her documents and the letter down on the table. Lillyann reached and grabbed them. She looked up and asked, "Mother, did you really try to kill my sister over money?" Lillyann started throwing it all at Saralee before she ran off to her room to cry.

"Now look what you have done," yelled Saralee. "You have upset your sister. You will pay for that."

Saralee walked out of the room and came back with a gun. She walked toward Minni and said, "Yes, I was going to kill you. Your grandfather was going to give you everything, leaving me nothing. I was young, and you were only two years old. I should have done it before you were taken from my home, then I would not have to deal with this. If you had just shut up and let me be, I would not have to finish the job now."

Minni started walking to the door and said, "You won't get away with this again, Saralee. My driver will come in to check on me."

Saralee said, "No, this is how we are going to do this. You will go upstairs and apologize to your sister and tell her everything you said was just a misunderstanding. Then we will wait till your driver comes to the door, and you will tell him to leave and that you are staying the night. Is that clear?"

Minni looked at her and angrily said, "Crystal."

After she came back downstairs from talking to her sister, her mother was sitting in her living room waiting.

"Well, did she believe you?" asked Saralee.

"Yes," said Minni as she sat down.

A few moments later, Minni's driver rang the doorbell. Saralee stood behind her, holding the gun on Minni-Lane.

"Ma'am, are you okay?" asked the driver.

"Yes, sir, I'm fine. I'm going to stay overnight to spend time with my sister."

The driver agreed and left. Saralee started laughing. "Good girl, you have done what you were told. Now we are leaving."

Saralee and Minni took off in a hurry because Saralee did not want Lillyann to see her do anything. She knew if Lillyann knew what was going on, she would never forgive her. A few moments after they left, Lillyann ran downstairs and called the police.

"Hello, my name is Lillyann," she said. "I know why my sister disappeared, and if y'all don't come soon, she will be gone forever."

The police arrived, and Lillyann told them everything. But before Saralee left, she had thrown all the proof into the fireplace, so Lillyann had no hard evidence to show them. When asked by the police how she knew all that, she said, "Before my sister left, she came upstairs and told me everything that she said was true, and my mother had a gun."

At this point, they called Anthony. Before Anthony left to head to the Shelby mansion, he called that number that he had saved after Minni-Lane told him to. Minni's father answered.

"Hello, Minni. Is everything okay?"

After a few moments, Fred told Anthony everything and also said that he had found the lawyer and butler, and they were ready to testify against Saralee.

"But Saralee had burned all your documents," said Anthony.

"Well, that's what Lillyann thinks what happened because they're gone. We have no proof," Fred said. "It will be okay if we have two witnesses to testify."

They all met at the police station, including the butler and lawyer. The case was going to be dismissed without having real proof rather than just hearsay. At that moment, the lawyer and butler opened their suitcases with the same documents and letters and a few other things from Minni's grandfather.

So now the search for Minni was on yet again for the third time so far.

"I will find her," said Fred. "That's my daughter, and I will not let Saralee hurt her."

Anthony was still trying to process everything. He was scared and worried about his love and didn't want anything to happen to her. Anthony yelled to start searching all of Saralee's properties and look in all the local woods, including where Minni grew up.

"We will not rest until she is home again!" he yelled as he got back in his car and began his search.

Lillyann was terrified and wanted to help search, but the police wouldn't allow it. She was only fourteen years old, and they felt they had to also protect her from Saralee. The police took Lillyann to the Chester family's mansion for her to stay there until they found Saralee. They did not want her home alone when Saralee got home because they were worried that when Saralee found out that Lillyann had called the police, she might hurt Lillyann as well.

The police took Lillyann to Anthony's house and had four police officers watching the house in case Minni or Saralee showed up. Lillyann sat in Minni's room with Bailey and just kept saying, "Why? Why would my mother do this? I really hope my sister is okay! What is going to happen when they find them? Is my sister going to be, okay?"

Bailey told her to calm down and said the police would bring Minni home safe (she was hoping).

"Go to bed," Bailey said as she tucked her in Minni's bed.

After a few moments, Lillyann fell asleep, and Bailey joined everyone to search for Minni-Lane Rose, the missing girl, again.

# Chapter 9

Saralee arrived back at her home. She searched the house for Lillyann, but she was gone. Saralee called Lillyann while she was with the Chester family. Lillyann answered and put it on speakerphone so the police could also hear what was being said.

"Hello," said Lillyann.

Her mother responded, "Where are you? Why did you leave without telling me where you were going?"

Lillyann replied, "I'm fine. I'm with the Chester family trying to find Minni."

Saralee took a deep breath and said, "Well, she probably ran off with that man that she thinks is her father."

"No, Mom," said Lillyann. "I know she left with you, and you are going to tell me where you took her right now!"

As they were on the phone, Saralee stayed calm. She knew that she had thrown the documents away, so she felt that there was no proof that she was the one who took Minni-Lane.

As Saralee was on the phone with Lillyann, the police showed up. They started reading her rights. Saralee just kept laughing, saying, "I have nothing to do with this, and without evidence, y'all can't do anything, so I suggest you let me go before I get my lawyer involved."

The police just ignored her and put her in the police car. They arrived at the police station and walked her to Officer Channing's office.

Officer Channing asked, "Where is Minni-Lane?"

Saralee looked at him and said, "Why would I know her whereabouts? She hardly comes to see me. Why don't you get ahold of that Fred man that took her in the beginning, because I have no idea where she would be."

Officer Channing said, "Let me give you one more time to tell me the truth. Your daughter saw her leaving with you right after Minni accused you of trying to murder her."

"That's ridiculous," said Saralee as she looked away. "I spent most of my life looking for her. Why would I have searched for her if I wanted her gone?"

"I have reason to believe that you are in fact the reason Annalee Rose Shelby went missing," said the officer.

"How so?" asked Saralee. "I want to see hardcore evidence to why you would believe that I would even think about harming one of my children."

Officer Channing yelled out, "Debbie, can you please send in the first set of witnesses?"

Saralee took a deep breath and gasped when she saw Kevin Foster, her father's butler, and Hyde Gammon, her father's lawyer.

"What are y'all doing here?" she asked.

The police then showed her all the documents that were originally from her father, Jason Shelby.

"You see, Ms. Shelby," said the officer, "your father was a very smart man. He made sure he sent those documents to multiple people. In fact, Kevin is the main witness from when you planned Annalee's death. He heard everything. Now, Ms. Shelby, I'm going to ask you one more time: where is Minni-Lane?"

Saralee looked around the room and said, "I have no idea what these men are talking about. Everything they just said was a lie. I want to speak to my lawyer right now!" she yelled.

As she looked up, she turned pale white when she thought she had seen a ghost. Minni's father walked into the office and said, "Hello, Saralee. Where is my daughter?"

"So you really are alive," said Saralee as she stood up. "I figured that my father would have just hired someone to pretend they were you, but it actually is you. You took my daughter and hid her and never told me the truth."

Minni's father looked at her with an odd and confused face and said, "Of course! Why would I tell someone that was trying to kill her where she was at?"

Saralee went to slap Fred. The officer jumped in and cuffed Saralee. The officer asked Fred if he would like to press charges for attempted murder. Fred nodded and said yes, then Fred looked at her one last time with tears in his eyes and asked, "Where is my daughter at?"

Saralee refused to answer until her lawyer was present.

Later that day, Saralee's lawyer, Aliyah, walked in and requested to speak to her client alone. After everyone walked out, Aliyah asked, "Is what they are saying the truth? I need to know if you really tried to kill your two-year-old baby over money?"

"What does it matter?" asked Saralee. "This is the present, not the past. Even if I did, it would not matter. I pay you very well, so stop with the questions and do your job and get me out of this."

Her lawyer, shocked she didn't even try to hide it, said, "Well, Saralee, I'm firing myself. I am no longer your lawyer, and I've already let everyone in my office know about you, and no one will agree to help you. You belong behind bars, Saralee, and that's where you shall go."

With Saralee not having a lawyer and still refusing to admit what had happened, they still had no idea where Minni-Lane was. At this point, they weren't even convinced she was alive; all they could do was search for her once again. So the police officer decided to have Lillyann go in there and try to get answers. After they begged her for a little while, Lillyann agreed to go talk to her mother.

A little while later, Lillyann walked in and said, "Where is my sister? Why did you do this? You never loved me. I was just a replacement for Minni-Lane."

Her mother looked at her and said, "That's nonsense. You are not a replacement. I love you. You were the one that was meant to be my child, not her. She was trying to take our whole life away from us because she has gotten selfish. If she would have stayed in her lane, then I would not have to be doing this."

Lillyann looked at her mother, confused, and yelled, "Of course she came after you! You tried to kill her over a silly inheritance. That is the worst that could happen to an innocent child. Now tell me, where is my sister?"

"Lillyann, do you remember when I took you a few states over to the beach? You had so much fun. You kept a smile on your face the whole weekend."

"So?" said Lillyann. "What does that have to do with my sister?"

Saralee looked at her and said, "I just want us to be able to have fun like that again."

Lillyann muttered "never again" under her breath, then shouted, "You are a murderer. You tried killing a two-year-old over money. I will never forgive you for that, and I want nothing to do with you anymore. I will be living with the Chester family until we find my sister. You are nothing to me!"

Saralee laughed and said, "Okay, Lillyann, good luck on finding Annalee, the missing girl, again."

Meanwhile, a few states down, Minni-Lane was tied down and hidden in the woods. Her mother thought that would be funny considering almost her whole life so far, she had been hidden in the woods. Only this time, she was tied up in a port-a-potty behind her mother's secret cabin. It was hot, and she had now been missing for a few days. Saralee had been in jail, so Minni had not had food or water. She was passing in and out due to the heat in there and barely any air going in through the cracks of the door. Minni-lane did not cry or struggle to get out. She just kept thinking, *Oh great, this is how I die—on a freaking toilet. This just in, missing rich girl dies sitting on a toilet in a port-a-potty hidden in the woods. I'm going to be the laughingstock all over the news. Man, I hope Saralee just buries me.* She was passing out again.

Minni-Lane's father and her sweet Anthony did not give up. They got permission from Lillyann to search their mansion for any and all clues they could find to see if she happened to have a place hidden or knew someone with a property hidden where she might have taken Minni-Lane. After searching every room and safe in that house, they found three possible properties where she might have taken Minni-Lane.

Minni's father contacted Lillyann and asked her about these properties that Saralee had. He said, "There's supposedly one in Mexico, one in Florida, and the other one is not too far from here by the beach."

Lillyann took a moment to think about it. Then she said, "Well, the one in Mexico is more of an apartment building full of residents. The one in Florida is her other beach house. We just went up there last year. It has renters right now. The other beach house we haven't gone to in years, and I believe that one is empty right now. Oh wait, my mother just asked me the other day if I remember this place, and it was right after I had asked her where my sister was. That's it. She must be there. That has to be it. Why else would my mother bring that up? I have the keys to that property. Do you want to meet up at my mother's house so that I can give them to you?"

"Yes please," said Minni's father. "If we can meet in an hour, I'm going to talk to the police right now."

An hour later, everybody met up at Saralee's house. Lillyann walked up to them and said, "Here are the keys to the beach house."

Fred asked, "What is the second one for?"

Lillyann said, "Oh, that's the key for her port-a-potty behind the house."

Everyone thanked Lillyann for all her cooperation in all the craziness that was going on. Lillyann said, "Thank you," as she looked down. Then she asked Fred, "Please bring my sister home safely."

A few hours later, they found the cabin in the woods. They searched the whole cabin from top to bottom, but they could not find Minni-Lane anywhere. Minni managed to wake up when she heard people over there around the house. It was hard to scream out due to the heat and being dehydrated, but she tried. "Help me, I'm back here!"

Anthony asked everyone to be quiet because he thought he had heard something.

"Help me! I'm back here."

Anthony yelled back, "Keep calling me so I can find you."

They ran to the back and saw the port-a-potty and asked, "Minni-Lane, are you in there?"

Barely able to breathe, she said, "Yes."

Minni-Lane's father busted the door open. Minni started to tear up when she saw her father standing in front of her. She said, "Father, I'm sorry I didn't believe you at first, and thank you for finding me."

Fred grabbed his daughter and hugged her closely while Anthony went to call for an ambulance because Minni was barely breathing and practically dead.

# Chapter 10

Months later, Minni-Lane was released from the hospital. She had bruises on her, and mentally, she was completely broken. The day she was released, she asked if her father, Fred, could be the one to pick her up. It had been a while since she had been able to have one-on-one time with him. When her father arrived, she ran to him with tears in her eyes and wrapped her arms around his neck to hug him.

They talked on the way back to the Chester family's mansion about her fourteen years in the woods and everything she had been through since she met Anthony. She was happy with how her life was changing now that her mother was out of the picture, and her father was back, trying to be the good father Minni-Lane deserved.

As they arrived at the mansion, the whole Chester family was standing outside, waiting for Minni to finally be home. Bailey was the first one to run up to Minni and hug her.

"Are you feeling okay?" asked Bailey. "Do you need anything? Shall I have Sue run you a bath?"

Minni just smiled and said, "Oh my, I have missed you."

Bailey said, "Hey, we have to plan this wedding since we had to cancel the first."

Minni ran into the house with her future sister-in-law to get started on getting this wedding over with.

There was now a lot to get done—first her wedding, then figuring out all her properties and finances. After she got married, she was going to finally take over her grandfather's business. She was eager to get back to living her life, only this time, she was rich with a career. But the most important thing was getting guardianship over her fourteen-year-old sister.

The next morning, Minni-Lane went to her mansion. She wanted to have the house put back to what it looked like when her grandfather was alive. She hired Kevin, her grandfather's butler, to come back and coordinate where everything should be, considering he knew that mansion better than anyone because he had lived and worked there for thirty years for Minni's grandfather.

Kevin met her there and asked, "Shall I have the maids go fetch all of your grandfather's belongings from the basement and have them start getting the mansion back to where it was today?"

Minni-Lane nodded her head and said, "Yes, and also donate all of Saralee's belongings. I do not want to be reminded of my mother."

As a few days went by, the mansion was finally once again the Shelby Mansion. Lillyann even loved the new-yet-old remodel that they had worked so hard to do.

Lillyann asked Minni, "Are we moving back in here after you are married? Or are we going to live with Anthony at his family's house?"

Minni looked at Lillyann with a confused face and said, "You know what, I haven't really put thought into that. I will talk to Anthony, and we will agree on where we are moving to after the wedding. And as soon as we know, I will let you know."

It was just a few days before Minni-Lane's wedding. She had gotten so much done at this point, including figuring out where they were going to be living after the wedding. Minni-Lane decided to have a family meeting with Anthony, Lillyann, and her father, Fred. She announced to her father and sister that the decision had been made on what was going to happen after the wedding: they would all move back into her grandfather's mansion.

Minni stood up and said, "I'm the guardian of Lillyann until her eighteenth birthday. Then I will split all the properties, business, and fortune equally with my sister. But for now, she will live with me, and I will raise her as my own. Also, Father, you will live here with us, and I will have you come work at my building."

Her father smiled and agreed with her decision. Fred said, "As long as I always know my daughter is safe, I will live anywhere to be near you."

Anthony also agreed that it would be a wonderful idea now that there was nothing left of Saralee in their home.

Minni-Lane had already bought her dress. It had a long train and was tight on her breasts and waist with a small flow at the bottom. It was off the shoulder, with long sleeves and rose patterns sewn on the dress. Minni was so proud of her dress; she'd designed it herself. Her sister's maid-of-honor dress had daisy flowers sewn onto hers. It was long, to her feet, also off the shoulder, with long sleeves, and it was sky blue to match the centerpieces, which were blue roses with gold ribbon in a fancy vase, also Minni-Lane's design. Minni was so happy with her designs that she even thought about opening her own fashion studio.

It was time for their wedding. Minni had been waiting to marry Anthony ever since they first met in the woods when she was sixteen. Minni knew she wanted to spend the rest of her life with Anthony; this was the best decision that she had ever made.

It was time to walk down the aisle. Minni took a deep breath as her father walked up to her to give her away to Anthony. The music started, and they began to walk into the church. Anthony looked up as his bride walked in. He could not help but stare at this amazing woman as she walked to him.

The preacher asked who would give Minni's hand in marriage. Fred proudly said, "I do." Then he handed his baby girl to her groom and went to sit down.

They insisted that they didn't want a traditional wedding. They wanted to make their own vows, and they wanted the ceremony to be short. Anthony began to say, "From the first moment I laid my eyes on you, I knew I was going to marry you. After spending the last several years searching for you, I know this is the best thing I will ever do. I promise to love you until death do us part."

Minni nervously cleared her throat and said, "Anthony, you have stolen my heart since the first day I looked into your dark brown eyes. There was something inside me that I had never felt before. I promise to love you until death do us part."

The preacher proudly said, "I now pronounce you Mr. and Mrs. Anthony Chester." The preacher looked at Anthony and said, "Now you may kiss your bride."

Anthony grabbed Minni's hand and pulled her quickly to him, tilting her while he kissed her as if they had never kissed before.

They walked out of the church and hugged their families. They left in a limo to head back to the Chester family's mansion to join everyone at the reception. When they arrived at the reception, the sun was setting, and it was absolutely beautiful. They had the reception in the backyard, and there were lights hanging everywhere with lit candles on all the tables. Minni-Lane finally felt as if she belonged and there was a meaning to her life. She felt as if she was now unstoppable. She had her grandfather's business and her family. All she ever really wanted was a family surrounded by love. She was ready to see where her life would take her now.

As everyone was enjoying themselves, Minni-Lane's father walked up to her and said, "I'm really happy that you met Anthony. It messed up your grandfather's and my plans for you taking over, but it still happened. Saralee is getting the justice she deserves, and I'm just really thankful that I can have the relationship with you that I always wanted and just be your dad."

Minni looked up at her father and said, "Daddy, I love you, and I'm thankful that you did what you did, and I do understand now why you did all of that. But we can be normal now. Let's just focus on the future rather than the past."

As her father held her close, he sang, "The storm will not last, it will soon fade. I will always be here to protect you till my very last day."

Minni held her father close as they danced.

In the woods behind the mansion, someone was hidden, looking at the party. What were they looking at, and who was this person? Most importantly, why was that person here?

"I will get you," said the mystery person.

Lillyann was dancing with her brother-in-law and looked over into the woods and saw something moving. She said, "Anthony, I think someone is out there."

Anthony reassured her it was probably an animal, and they continued dancing.

The party was over, and Anthony and Minni-Lane left in their limo for the airport to begin their honeymoon. And that is how the mystery girl was now found.

The end

# About The Author

Randi Stroyan was born in Texas. She's a great mother to her three children and five stepchildren and loves to tell them authentic stories.

www.ingramcontent.com/pod-product-compliance
Lightning Source LLC
Chambersburg PA
CBHW021141130726
47988CB00003B/1404